The Ultimate Dad Jokes That Will Make You Laugh Out Loud!
500+ Jokes and Puns

Dr. Chad Williams
FunLifeNow

Copyright © 2022
Dr. Chad Williams / Fun Life Now L.L.C.
FunLifeNow.Com

This book is a work of humor and is intended for entertainment purposes only.

All brand names and product names used in this book are trademarks, registered trademarks, or trade names of their respective holders. Fun Life Now L.L.C., is not associated with any product or vendor in this book. Although the author and publisher have made every effort to ensure that the information in this book was correct at press time, the author and publisher do not assume and hereby disclaim any liabilities to any party for any loss, damage, or disruption caused by errors or omissions, whether such errors or omissions result from negligence, or any other case.

No part of this publication may be reproduced, stored in a retrieval system, or transmitted in any form by any means electronic, mechanical, recording, or otherwise without the prior permission of the Copywrite owner.

Book Cover Jacket Created and Designed by:
KingOf_Designer
https://www.fiverr.com/kingof_designer

All rights reserved.

ISBN: 9798361883486

FunLifeNow - We are all about embracing the blending of custom personalized artwork, books, and just silly fun items. Whatever creative pursuit you are looking to begin or revisit with fresh eyes we hope to bring enjoyment to you.

You Have One Life. Live It.

WE NEED YOUR HELP:
We would greatly appreciate you taking a few moments to review this book.
Your efforts will help us to grow and bring further enjoyment to others.

Titles also Available by FunLifeNow:

- Personal Gratitude Journal: Bring Meaning to the Day, daily 5-Minute Guide for Mindfulness, Positivity, and Self Care
- 3 Column Ledger Book: Accounting Journal Ledger Book
- 4 Column Ledger Book: Accounting Journal Ledger Book
- 6 Column Ledger Book: Accounting Journal Ledger Book
- Ledger Book: Record Income and Expenses
- The Ultimate Dad Jokes That Will Make You Laugh Out Loud! 500+ Jokes and Puns Volume 2
- The Ultimate Collection: 300+ Brain Riddles and Read-Out Loud Jokes
- Random, Wild, and Unusual Fun Facts: 1000+ mind-blowing trivia facts
- Random, Wild, and Unusual Fun Facts: 1000+ mind-blowing trivia facts Volume 2
- Would You? Could You Questions: Travel and Party Fun
- 1500 Sudoku Books: Entertain and Challenge the Brian Series Volumes 1 – 10
- And more……

"You don't stop laughing because you grow older. You grow older because you stop laughing."

- Maurice Chevalier

1. What do you call a cow with two legs?

   » Lean beef.

   What if the cow has no legs?

   » ground beef.

2. What is the best way to watch a fly-fishing tournament?

   » Live stream of course.

3. What group of people never gets angry?

   »Nomads

4. What do you call two married monkeys who have an Amazon account?

   » Prime mates.

5. I used to shower at night, then I started showering in the morning. The difference was night and day.

6. **What did the duck say when it bought ChapStick?**

   » "Put it on my bill."

7. **I am Buzz Aldrin. Second man to step on the moon. Neil before me.**

8. **I told my wife she needs to start embracing her mistakes.**

   So then turned and hugged me.

9. **Why can't you send a duck to space?**

   » Because the bill would be astronomical.

10. **What does a cow use to do math?**

    » A cow-culator.

11. **How deep is the water in the lake?**

    » Chest deep on a duck

12. **Why do hummingbirds hum?**

    » Because they don't know the words.

13. **Why did Han Solo not enjoy his steak dinner last night?**

    » It was Chewie.

14. **My son chewed on an electrical cord today. Due to his current conduct, I had to ground him.**

15. **I got fired from my job as a taxi driver. It turns out customers do not appreciate when you go the extra mile.**

16. **Why was it so windy in the stadium?**

    » There were a bunch of fans.

17. **Where do boats go when they're sick?**

    » To the dock.

18. **Can February March?**

    » No, but April May.

19. **I named my golden retriever dog "4 miles." That way I could frequently say, "I am going to walk 4 miles now."**

20. **Why did the Clydesdale give the pony a glass of water?**

    » Because he was a little horse.

21. **What did one hat say to the other?**

    » Stay here! I'm going on ahead.

22. **How do you organize an outer space party?**

    » You planet.

23. **Did you hear about the French general who stepped on a landmine?**

    » His name was Napoleon Blown Apart.

24. **Why did an old man fall into a well?**

    » Because he could not see that well.

25. **My wife told me to pick up 8 cans of soda on my way home from work………She was pretty mad when I only picked seven up**

26. **Do you want to hear a joke about paper?**

    » Never mind—it's tearable.

27. **I went to a seafood dance last week… and pulled a mussel.**

28. **Why don't restaurants serve noodles after 11:00 PM?**

   ≫ It's pasta bedtime.

29. **How can a leopard change his spots?**

   ≫ By moving.

30. **Where do bad rainbows go?**

   ≫ Prism. It is just a light sentence.

31. **Why do balloons dislike Michael Jackson?**

   ≫ They are afraid of pop music.

32. **How do lawyers say goodbye?**

   ≫ We will be suing ya.

33. **Where does bread rise?**

   ≫ In the Yeast.

34. **Spring is here!**

    ⫸ I got so excited I got to wet my plants.

35. **Did you hear about the actor that fell through the floorboards?**

    ⫸ He was just going through a stage.

36. **What happens when you do not pay an exorcist?**

    ⫸ You get repossessed.

37. **How do you get the neighbor's farm daughter to like you?**

    ⫸ A tractor

38. **What do you get when you cross a snail with a porcupine?**

    ⫸ A slowpoke

39. **Why do chicken coops only have two doors?**

    》 Because if they had four, they would be chicken sedans.

40. **Whenever we drive past a graveyard my father says,
'Do you know why I can't be buried there?'
And we all say, 'Why not?'
And he says, 'Because I'm not dead yet.**

41. **A hen will always leave her house through the proper eggs-it.**

42. **Why did the cookie cry?**

    》 Because his father was a wafer so long.

43. **The man who ate too many eggs was considered to be an egg-oholic.**

44. Why couldn't the pony sing "Happy Birthday?"

    》 Because she was just a little hoarse.

45. What do you call a belt with a watch on it?

    》 A waist of time.

46. How do you keep a bull from charging?

    》 Take away its credit card.

47. All the hens consider the chef to be a very mean person.

    It is because he beats the eggs.

48. My wife just completed a 40-week bodybuilding program this morning.

    It's a girl and weighs 6lbs 9 oz.

49. Eskimos keep all of their chilled eggs inside of the egg-loo.

50. Something to ponder…What would bears be without the letter B?

    »› Ears.

51. The best time of day to eat eggs is at the crack of dawn.

52. Why does Dracula always bite people in the neck?

    »› Because he's a neck romancer

53. I know a bunch of good jokes about umbrellas, but they usually go over people's heads.

54. Of all the inventions of the last 100 years, the dry-erase board it has to be the most remarkable.

55. **Do you know the story about the chicken that crossed the road?**

   » Me neither, I couldn't follow it.

56. **How many narcissists does it take to screw in a light bulb?**

   » One. The narcissist holds the light bulb while the rest of the world revolves around him.

57. **What kind of socks do grizzlies wear?**

   » None, they have bear feet.

58. **The day I turned 42, my daughter walked up to me and said "happy...", and started timing on her watch.**

   After a long silence, she said "...40 second birthday."

59. What is the most popular fish in the ocean?

    ≫ A starfish.

60. Today, my son asked "Can I have a bookmark?" and I burst into tears. 11 years old and he still doesn't know my name is Brian.

61. I don't trust stairs.
    They are always up to something.

62. I failed math so many times at school, I can't even count.

63. Dad, will you put my shirt on?

    ≫ No, it won't fit me.

64. When I was a kid, my dad got fired from his job as a road worker for theft. I refused to believe he could do such a thing, but when I got home, the signs were all there.

65. **I bet Benjamin Franklin was shocked when he discovered electricity.**

66. **I used to have a handle on life, but then it broke.**

67. **How did the telephone propose?**

    » With a ring.

68. **What invention allows us to see through walls?**

    » Windows.

69. **Don't you hate it when someone answers their own questions?**

    » I do.

70. What kind of people man a haunted ship?

    » A skeleton crew.

71. The problem with kleptomaniacs is that they always take things literally.

72. Two conspiracy theorists walk into a shop. …..
    That can't be a coincidence.

73. My wife just found out I replaced our bed with a trampoline.
    She hit the ceiling.

74. Where do polar bears keep their money?

    » In a snow bank

75. Are people born with photographic memories, or does it take time to develop?

76. What's worse than raining cats and dogs?

    » Hailing taxis.

77. Why was the pig covered in ink?

    » Because of course, it lived in a pen.

78. A book fell on my head the other day. I only have my shelf to blame though.

79. Did you know you can hear your blood flowing in your veins?

    You just need to listen varICOSEly.

80. I told my daughter, "Go to bed, the cows are sleeping in the field."

    She said, "What's that got to do with anything?"

    I said, "That means it's pasture bedtime."

81. What does a mobster buried in cement soon become?

    》 A hardened criminal.

82. How often did my friend drive his DeLorean?

    》 From time to time

83. A man walks into a pet store and asks for a dozen bees. The clerk carefully counts 13 bees out onto the counter. "That's one too many!" says the customer. The clerk replies, "It's a freebie."

84. **What do you get when dinosaurs crash their cars?**

    » Tyrannosaurus wrecks.

85. **Barbers…
    you have to take your hat off to them.**

86. **What did the sink say to the toilet?**

    » You look flushed.

87. **What did one plate say to another plate?**

    » Tonight, dinner's on me.

88. **Russian dolls are so full of themselves.**

89. **Did you hear about the surgeon who enjoyed performing quick surgeries on insects?**

    » He mainly did them on the fly.

90. **What building has the most stories?**

    » A library.

91. **The easiest time to add an insult to injury is when you're signing someone's cast.**

92. **Why are ghosts, such bad liars?**

    » You can see right through them.

93. **Why is a snake difficult to fool?**

    » You can't pull its leg.

94. **Where do dogs hate shopping?**

    » A flea market.

95. **My therapist says I have a preoccupation for revenge. We'll see about that.**

96. What's green with six legs and will crush you if it falls on you?

    » A pool table.

97. Which vegetable do sailors hate the most?

    » Leeks

98. Light travels faster than sound, which is the reason that some people appear bright before you hear them speak.

99. What's a cat's favorite dessert?

    » Chocolate mouse

100. People who use selfie sticks really need to have a good, long look at themselves.

101. **What fish only swims at night?**

    » Starfish

102. **What do you get if you cross an angry sheep with a moody cow?**

    » An animal that's in a Baaaaaaaaad Moooooooood.

103. **The magazine about ceiling fans went out of business due to low circulation.**

104. **Why are snails bad at racing?**

    » They're sluggish.

105. **The chicken coop only had 2 doors since it would be a sedan if it had 4 doors.**

106. **Crossing a cement mixer and a chicken will result in you getting a brick layer.**

107. **Why do seagulls fly over the sea?**

    If they flew over the bay, they'd be called bagels.

108. **People using umbrellas always seem to be under the weather.**

109. **Can a high jumper jump higher than the Empire State Building?**

    ≫ Of course! Buildings can't jump.

110. **Where do you imprison a skeleton?**

    In a rib cage.

111. **I went to buy some camouflage trousers the other day – but I couldn't find any.**

112. **How do you get a squirrel to like you?**

    ≫ Act like a nut.

113. **The soundtrack for Finding Nemo was ORCAstrated.**

114. **Why don't eggs tell jokes?**

    » They'd crack each other up.

115. **I really look up to my tall friends.**

116. **Can a kangaroo jump higher than the Empire State Building?**

    » Of course! The Empire State Building can't jump.

117. **Don't ever have multiple people wash dishes together.
It's hard for them to stay in sink.**

118. What do you call malware on a Kindle?

    ≫ A bookworm.

119. A group of aquatic mammals at the zoo escaped.

    It was otter chaos!

120. I have a clean conscience — it's never been used.

121. What do you do to an open wardrobe?

    ≫ You closet.

122. You see my next-door neighbor worshiping exhaust pipes,.........

    He is a Catholic converter.

123. **What did the alpaca say to his date?**

   » "Want to go on a picnic? Alpaca lunch."

124. **I dissected an iris today.
It was an eye-opening experience.**

125. **Why was the belt sent to jail?**

   » For holding up a pair of pants.

126. **Where do you find a cow with no legs?**

   » Where ever you left it

127. **What do you call a baby monkey?**

   » A chimp off the old block.

128. **Two peanuts were walking down the street.**

   Unfortunately, one was a salted.

129. **Do you think glass coffins will be a success?**

   » Remains to be seen.

130. **How do you tell the difference between a frog and a horny toad?**

   » A frog says, 'Ribbit, ribbit' and a horny toad says, 'Rub it, rub it.

131. **What lies at the bottom of the ocean and twitches?**

   » A nervous wreck.

132. **What do you call Bill Gates when he is flying?**

   » Bill-in-air

133. **What happens when a frog's car dies?**

   》 He needs a jump and if that does not work he has to get it toad.

134. **Long fairy tales have a tendency to dragon.**

135. **What do you call a flying priest?**

   A bird of pray

136. **What planet is like a circus?**

   》 Saturn, it has three rings.

137. **Did you hear about the scientist who was a lab partner with a pot of boiling water?**

   》 He was a very esteemed colleague.

138. **Why are bakers so rich?**

    » They make a lot of dough

139. **Where do terrorists go when they die?**

    » Everywhere

140. **If a child doesn't want to take a nap, are they guilty of resisting a rest?**

141. **Which cat is the least loyal?**

    » A cheetah

142. **What room can no one enter?**

    » A mushroom

143. **What is blue and not very heavy?**

    » Light blue

144. I used to have a calendar factory job but got fired because I took a couple of days off.

145. What is a witch's favorite way to write?

    ≫ Cursive

146. Before my father died he worked in a circus as a stilt walker.

    ≫ I used to look up to him.

147. What do you call a zombies butt?

    ≫ Deadass

148. Why was 2019 afraid of 2020?

    ≫ Because they had a fight and 2021.

149. What is the easiest way to burn 1000 calories?

    ≫ Leave dinner on the BBQ for too long.

150. **Why did the lion eat the tightrope walker?**

   ≫ He wanted a well-balanced meal

151. **Why should you never trust a goldfish's excuse?**

   ≫ They always seem a little fishy.

152. **It takes guts to make a sausage.**

153. **What do you call a penguin wondering around in the White House?**

   ≫ Lost.

154. **I always take life with a grain of salt. And a slice of lemon. And a shot of tequila.**

155. **What's brown and sounds like a bell?**

   ≫ Dung

156. **Did you hear about the cat who ate a ball of yarn?**

    » She had mittens.

157. **What do you call a kangaroo's lazy joey?**

    » A pouch potato.

158. **What kind of room doesn't have doors?**

    » A mushroom.

159. **How does a boar sign its name?**

    » With a pig pen.

160. **Just burned 2,000 calories. That's the last time I leave brownies in the oven as I take a nap.**

161. **Where do baby cats learn to swim?**

    ≫ The kitty pool.

162. **Who has been spreading rumors?**

    ≫ Butter.

163. **Which is faster, hot or cold?**

    ≫ Hot, because you can catch a cold.

164. **I searched for a lighter on Amazon, but all I could find were 5,000 matches.**

165. **What did the photon say when asked if she needed to check a bag?**

    ≫ "No thanks, I'm traveling light"

166. **What do you say to boiling water?**

    ≫ You'll be mist.

167. Did you hear about the crustacean accused of promoting his own shellfish interests?

168. The problem isn't that obesity runs in your family. It's that no one runs in your family.

169. Did you hear about the shepherd who drove his sheep through town and was given a ticket for making a ewe turn?

170. Why did the astronaut leave the party?

    »» He needed a little space.

171. Why did the triangle feel sorry for the circle?

    »» Because it's pointless

172. Why do people take extra socks when golfing?

    » They might get a hole in one.

173. Always borrow money from a pessimist……..They'll never expect it back.

174. Did you hear about the bankrupt poet who ode everyone?

175. I don't suffer from insanity—I enjoy every minute of it.

176. What instrument can you find in the bathroom?

    » A tuba toothpaste.

177. Today a man knocked on my door and asked for a small donation toward the local swimming pool. I gave him a glass of water.

178. **What do sprinters eat before a race?**

    » Nothing because they fast.

179. **A ghost walked into a bar and ordered a shot of vodka. The bartender said, 'Sorry, we don't serve spirits here.'**

180. **What did the pizza say to the topping?**

    » I never sau-sage a pretty face

181. **I threw a boomerang a couple of years ago; I know live in constant fear.**

182. **Why was the rookie police officer assigned to hunt the cannibal?**

    » The more seasoned officers had already been eaten.

183. Did you hear about the guy whose whole left side got amputated?

   » He's all right now.

184. What did the bunny say to the carrot?

   » It's been nice gnawing you

185. I saw a sign the other day that said, 'Watch for children,' and I thought, 'That sounds like a fair trade.'

186. A cheese factory exploded in France. Da brie is everywhere

187. What did one dried fruit say when another asked it to the movies?

   » It's a date

188. **Did you hear about the guy who stole 50 cartons of hand sanitizer?**

    They couldn't prosecute—his hands were clean.

189. **I have a few jokes about unemployed people, but none of them work.**

190. **What kind of key opens a banana?**

    » A mon-key

191. **What does garlic do when it gets hot?**

    » It takes its cloves off

192. **A blind man walked into a bar… and a table… and a chair…**

193. **Where does fruit go on vacation?**

    » Pear-is

194. It's a shame that the Beatles didn't make the submarine in that song green. ….

    That would've been sublime.

195. Why couldn't the angle get a loan?

    » Because his parents wouldn't cosine

196. We have spent a lot of time, money, and effort childproofing our house, but the kids still get in.

197. Did you hear the one about the kid who started a business tying shoelaces on the playground?

    » It was a knot-for-profit.

198. What kind of car business would Yoda start?

    » A Toy Yoda dealership

199. It's a 5-minute walk from my house to the bar, but a 45-minute walk from the bar to my house.

   The difference is staggering

200. A baby's laugh is one of the most beautiful things you will ever hear. Unless it is 2 a.m., you don't have a baby and you are home alone.

201. Where did Luke Skywalker buy his new arm?

   » At the second hand store

202. My landlord texted saying we need to meet up and talk about how high my heating bill is.

   I replied back: "Sure, my door is always open."

203. **What was Luke's reaction to food made by baby Wookiees?**

"It's good, but it's a little Chewie."

204. **I caught my son chewing on electrical cords, so I had to ground him. He's doing better currently, and now conducting himself properly.**

205. **Why does Darth Vader always sound so angry when he breathes?**

   » He's always venting.

206. **Do you know what a baby computer calls his old man?**

   » Data.

207. **What was Luke's secret codename before he got his mechanical limb?**

   » Hand Solo

208. **Why do we dress babies in onesies? Because they can't dress themselves.**

209. **Where would Darth Vader stay if he would settle down in the USA?**

    » The Empire State Building.

210. **Did you hear about the claustrophobic astronaut?**

    » He just wanted a little more space.

211. **Who's bigger? Mrs. Bigger, Mr. Bigger, or their baby?**

    » Their baby — because he's a little Bigger.

212. **Did you hear they arrested the devil?**

    Yeah, they got him on possession.

213. **What do you call Chewbacca when he has chocolate stuck in his fur?**

    ›› A chocolate chip Wookie.

214. **What do you call 50,000 female pigs and 50,000 male deer?**

    100 sows and bucks.

215. **Which Star Wars character works at a restaurant?**

    ›› Darth Waiter

216. **Why do cows wear bells?**

    ›› Because their horns don't work.

217. **How did Darth Vader know what Luke was getting for his birthday?**

    ›› He felt his presents.

218. **Police arrested a bottle of water because it was wanted in three different states:**

solid, liquid, and gas.

219. **Why did the Jedi cross the road?**

》 To get to the dark side.

220. **Why is grass so dangerous?**

》 Because it's full of blades.

221. **What is Jabba the Hutt's middle name?**

》 The

222. **What is the Easter bunny's favorite type of music?**

》 Hip-hop.

223. How can you tell if a snake is a baby?

    » It has a rattle.

224. What's the leading cause of dry skin?

    » Towels

225. Did you know milk is the fastest liquid on earth?

    » It's pasteurized before you even see it.

226. Where did the dog go after losing its tail?

    » To the retail store

227. What did the 0 say to the 8?

    » "Nice belt."

218. Police arrested a bottle of water because it was wanted in three different states:

solid, liquid, and gas.

219. Why did the Jedi cross the road?

》 To get to the dark side.

220. Why is grass so dangerous?

》 Because it's full of blades.

221. What is Jabba the Hutt's middle name?

》 The

222. What is the Easter bunny's favorite type of music?

》 Hip-hop.

223. How can you tell if a snake is a baby?

    » It has a rattle.

224. What's the leading cause of dry skin?

    » Towels

225. Did you know milk is the fastest liquid on earth?

    » It's pasteurized before you even see it.

226. Where did the dog go after losing its tail?

    » To the retail store

227. What did the 0 say to the 8?

    » "Nice belt."

228. What do you call a duck who is addicted?

    » A quackhead

229. Do you want to hear a joke about construction?

    I'm still working on it.

230. What kind of tree fits into your hand?

    » A palm tree

231. The most amazing thing happened today. A magic tractor was driving down the road when it turned into a field

232. Where do boats go when they're sick?

    » To the boat doc.

233. **Did you hear the joke about the wandering nun?**

    》 She was a Roman Catholic.

234. **I got a little crazy and went to a seafood disco last Friday night.**

    That is when I pulled a mussel

235. **What do you call a typo on a headstone?**

    》 A grave mistake.

236. **What do you call two octopuses that look the same?**

    》 Itenticle.

237. **What did one ocean say to the other ocean?**

    》 Nothing, they just waved and waved and waved.

238. What did the fish say when he hit the wall?

   》 Dam!

239. Why did everyone enjoy being around the volcano?

   》 It's just so lava-ble.

240. What's the difference between a piano and a fish?

   》 You can tune a piano, but you can't tuna fish.

241. What kind of music do the planets listen to?

   》 Nep-tunes

242. How do you organize a space party?

   》 You planet.

243. A woman was 3 months pregnant when she fell into a deep coma and woke up after about 6 months.

The woman asked the doctor about her baby.

Doctor: You had twins, a boy, and a girl. They're both fine. And, your brother named them for you.

Woman: No! Not my brother. He's an idiot! What did he name the girl?

Doctor: Denise.

Woman: Ohh, that's a nice name. What about the boy?

Doctor: {takes a deep breath and says} Denephew.

244. **I relished the fact that you've mustard the strength to ketchup to me in the race.**

245. How did the baby know she was ready to be born?

    》 She was running out of womb.

246. I heard Donald Trump is going to ban shredded cheese and make America grate again.

247. What do you call a young musician?

    》 A minor.

248. Did you hear about the restaurant on the moon?

    》 Great food, no atmosphere.

249. My friend keeps saying "cheer up man it could be worse, you could be stuck underground in a hole full of water."

    I know he means well.

250. Hey what time is your appointment with the dentist?

    Tooth hurt-y

251. I just watched a program about beavers.

    It was the best dam program I've ever seen.

252. I changed my iPod name to Titanic. It's syncing now.

253. What was the hot chocolate's biggest fear?

    » Getting mugged.

254. Brad broke his finger today, but on the other hand, he was completely fine.

255. What did the fried rice say to the shrimp?

   》 Don't wok away from me.

256. I rubbed some ketchup all over my eyes last night.

   It was a bad idea in Heinz sight.

257. The secret service is not allowed to yell "Get down!" anymore when the president is about to be attacked.

   Now they must yell "Donald Duck!"

258. If artists wear sketchers
do linguists wear converse?

259. I flipped a coin over a pressing issue at work, it was quite the toss-up.

260. **Did you hear what the couple who were working at an instruction book company named their child?**

    » Manuel.

261. **Did you hear the one about the dog and the tree?**

    » They had a long conversation about bark.

262. **There was a dad who tried to keep his wife happy through labor by telling jokes, but she didn't laugh once. Know why?**

    » It was the delivery.

263. **My son was just born and another dad at the nursery congratulated me and said his daughter was born yesterday. He said:** maybe they'll marry each other. **I replied:** Sure, like my son is going to marry someone twice his age.

264. My daughter's boyfriend introduced himself to me and said, 'Hello, sir, I'm David. Nice to meet you.' He put out his hand and I said, 'David, are you nervous?' He said no, so I grabbed his hand, looked him in the eyes, and said, 'Then why are you shaking?'

265. What gets wetter the more it dries?

    》 A towel.

266. I am reading a book about anti-gravity.

    It is absolutely impossible to put down.

267. I was kidnapped by mimes once………..They did unspeakable things to me.

268. I asked my dad for his best dad joke, and he said, 'You.'

269. What do you call a fake noodle?

    » An impasta.

270. What do you call it when Batman skips church?

    » Christian Bale.

271. I do not trust atoms.......

    They make up everything

272. Hear about the new restaurant called Karma?

    There's no menu—you get what you deserve.

273. Why did the scarecrow win an award?

    » Because he was outstanding in his field.

274. **Did you hear the one about the dog and the tree?**

   » It turns out they had a long conversation about bark.

275. **What did the ranch dressing say when the refrigerator door was opened?**

   » Close the door, I'm dressing.

276. **Why do bees have sticky hair?**

   » Because they use a honeycomb.

277. **Knock, knock.**
   Who's there?
   Cargo.
   Cargo who?
   Car go, "Toot toot, vroom, vroom!"

278. **What is the opposite of a croissant?**

   » A happy uncle.

279. A three-legged dog walks into a western bar and says to the bartender,

    'I'm looking for the man who shot my paw.'

280. What did the coffee report to the police?

    》 A mugging.

281. Which branch of the military accepts toddlers?

    》 The infantry.

282. I made a pencil with two erasers.

    It was pointless.

283. Two antennas get married.
    The ceremony was rubbish – but the reception was amazing.

284. I could tell a joke about pizza, but it is a little cheesy.

285. What is an astronaut's favorite part of a computer?

    》 The space bar.

286. They all laughed when I said I wanted to be a comedian.

    Well, they're not laughing now! Hummm...

287. I told my daughter, 'Go to bed, the cows are sleeping in the field.'

    She said, 'What's that got to do with anything?'

    I said, 'That means it's pasture bedtime.'

288. I don't play soccer because I enjoy the sport.

   I am just playing it for kicks.

289. What's the difference between a poorly dressed man on a unicycle and a well-dressed man on a bicycle?

   ⫸ Attire.

290. Why are elevator jokes so classic and funny?

   ⫸ They work on so many levels.

291. My wife found out I was cheating on her after she found all the letters I was hiding...she got mad and said she's never playing Scrabble with me again.

292. Did you hear about the guy who invented the knock-knock joke?

   ⫸ He won the 'no-bell' prize.

293. What would you call the terminator after he retires?

   » Exterminator

294. What has five toes but isn't your foot?

   » My foot

295. Why are toilets so good at poker?

   » They are good at getting a flush

296. I broke up with my girlfriend of five years because I found out she was a communist.

   I should have known — there were red flags everywhere.

297. What do you get from a pampered cow?

   » Spoiled milk

298. Did you hear the news?
FedEx and UPS are merging.

They're going to go by the name Fed-Up from now on.

299. My wife asked me to flip the calendar to the next month. To my surprise, the calendar skipped from April to June.

I turned to tell her we were missing a month. She said, "What's the matter? You look dis-Mayed."

300. What do you call a zombie who is cooking stir frie?

>> Dead man wok-ing

301. What do you call a twitching cow?

>> Beef jerky.

302. I was just reminiscing about the beautiful herb garden I had when I was growing up. Good thymes.

303. What do you call a beehive without an exit?

    » UnBeeLeaveable.

304. How does the moon cut its hair?

    » Eclipse it.

305. My friend wants to become an archaeologist, but I'm trying to put him off.

    I'm convinced his life will be in ruins.

306. Why do ducks have so many tail feathers?

    » To cover up their butt quacks.

307. **What crime do blacksmiths most commonly get charged with?**

    » Forgery.

308. **My dog accidentally swallowed a bunch of Scrabble tiles.**

    I think this could spell disaster.

309. **To the person who stole my place in the queue.**

    I'm after you now.

310. **Why are skeletons so calm?**

    » Because nothing gets under their skin.

311. **I asked the librarian if books about paranoia were available.**

    She looked up and whispered, "They're right behind you".

312. My therapist told me I have problems with the verbalization of my emotions.

    I could not say "I am surprised".

313. If Ani is short for Anakin and Obi is short for Obi-Wan, what is Luke short for?

    ≫ A stormtrooper.

314. How do you get over claustrophobia?

    ≫ By thinking outside of the box.

315. I've been breeding racing deer.

    I am just trying to make a quick buck.

316. Why did the koala get the job?

    ≫ He was koalafied.

317. Doctor:
I think your DNA is backwards.

Me responding back to Doctor:
...AND?

318. How do doctors stay calm during an emergency?

    » They've got a lot of patients.

319. So what if I don't know what the word apocalypse means?

    It's not the end of the world.

320. Why does a geologist hate his job?

    » He's taken for granite.

321. What do clouds do when they become rich?

    » They make it rain

322. **What do you do if you're afraid of speed bumps?**

   » You slowly get over it.

323. **What's a bad wizard's favorite computer program?**

   » Spell check.

324. **Why shouldn't you make fun of a paleontologist?**

   » Because you will get Jurasskicked.

325. **What did Microsoft Office say to earn your trust?**

   » You have my Word.

326. **Karl Marx is a historically famous philosopher, but no one ever mentions his sister, Onya, the inventor of the starting pistol.**

327. **What did the big flower say to the tiny flower?**

   » "Hey there bud."

328. **What did Mars ask Saturn?**

   » "Hey, why don't you give me a ring sometime?"

329. **Want to hear a Potassium joke?**

   » K

330. **Why do flamingos only lift one leg?**

   » If they lifted both, they'd fall down.

331. **Why are helium, curium, and barium the medical elements?**

   » Because if you can't heal-ium or cure-ium, you bury-um.

332. **Can you drop an egg on concrete without cracking it?**

   » Of course. Concrete is pretty difficult to break.

333. **What's the fastest way to determine the sex of a chromosome?**

   » Pull down its genes

334. **How do you get over a fear of elevators?**

   » You take the necessary steps to avoid them.

335. **How did the chemist feel about oxygen and potassium hanging out?**

   » OK.

336. **A pirate walks into a bar with a paper towel on his head.**

   The bartender says, "What's with the paper towel?"

   The pirate says, "Arrrrrr! I've got a Bounty on my head!"

337. **How many apples grow on a tree?**

   » All of them.

338. **When Silver Surfer and Iron Man team up, what do you call them?**

   » Alloys.

339. **Why can't you trust a balloon?**

   » It's full of hot air.

340. **Why did Beethoven get rid of his chickens?**

   » All it said was, "Bach, Bach, Bach…"

341. **What is a snowman tantrum called?**

   » A meltdown.

342. **What did one DNA say to the other DNA?**

   » "Do these genes make me look fat?"

343. **Why are computers so intelligent?**

   » Because they listen to their motherboards.

344. **Did you hear about the restaurant on the moon?**

   » Great food, but it has no atmosphere.

345. Can one bird make a joke?

    » No, but toucan.

346. What did the skeleton order with its beer?

    » A mop.

347. What's red and bad for your teeth?

    » A brick.

348. Why do nurses like red crayons?

    » Sometimes they have to draw blood.

349. What has more letters than the alphabet?

    » The post office.

350. **What kind of spells do leprechauns use?**

    》 Lucky Charms.

351. **What's red and looks like half an apple?**

    》 Half an apple.

352. **3.14 percent of sailors are pi-rates.**

353. **How did the zombie bodybuilder hurt himself?**

    》 He was dead-lifting.

354. **I hate Russian Dolls, they are so full of themselves.**

355. **Did I tell you the time I fell in love during a backflip?**

    》 I was heels over head

356. In chemistry class I never understood odorless chemicals, they never make scents.

357. I tried to organize a professional hide-and-seek tournament, but it was a complete failure.

    Good players are hard to find.

358. What do you call an elephant that doesn't matter?

    》 An irrelephant.

359. There's a fine line between the numerator and the denominator.

360. I used to work as a hairdresser, but I just wasn't cut out for it.

361. The lumberjack loved his new computer. He especially enjoyed logging in.

362. I went to my doctor today and told him I was having problems with my hearing.

    He asked, 'Can you describe the symptoms?'

    I replied, 'Sure...they're yellow, Homer's slow and fat, and Marge has blue hair.'

363. Did you hear about the guy who invented Lifesavers?

    » They say he made a mint.

364. Why can't you hear a psychiatrist using the bathroom?

    » Because the 'P' is silent.

365. Why is metal and a microwave a match made in heaven?

    » When they met, sparks flew.

366. What do you get from a pampered cow?

    》 Spoiled milk.

367. I sat down for dinner at a restaurant, and the waiter asked me, 'Do you want to hear today's special?'

    I said, 'Yes, please,'

    so he replied, 'No problem, sir. Today is special.'

368. If a child refuses to sleep during nap time, are they guilty of resisting a rest?

369. Of all the inventions of the last 100 years, the dry-erase board must be the most remarkable.

370. I ordered a chicken and an egg online…… I'll let you know which comes first.

371. Lettuce take a moment to appreciate this salad pun.

372. It takes guts to be an organ donor.

373. Why was 2019 afraid of 2020?

    » Because they had a fight and 2021.

374. If you see a crime at an Apple Store, does that make you an iWitness?

375. What do prisoners use to call each other?

    » Cell phones.

376. Thinking about math did you know that the average person is really mean.

377. I'm so good at sleeping, I can do it with my eyes closed.

378. Dad, did you get a haircut?

"No, I got them all cut.

379. I took my 8-year-old to the office on Take Your Kid to Work Day. As we were walking around, she started crying and getting very cranky, so I asked her what was wrong as my coworkers gathered around, she sobbed, 'Daddy, where are all the clowns that you said you worked with?'

380. What happened when the magician got mad?

》 He pulled his hare out

381. I asked my date to meet me at the gym, but she never showed up.

Guess the two of us aren't going to work out.

382. Do you know why I like egg puns?

    They crack me up.

383. Whenever the cashier at the grocery store asks my dad if he would like the milk in a bag he replies, 'No, just leave it in the carton.'

384. When a clock is hungry, it goes back four seconds.

385. Nothing's better than being 2, 3, 5, 7, 11, 13, 17, 19, 23, 29, 31, 37, 41, 43, 47, 53, 59, 61, 67, 71, 73, 79, 83, 89, or 97 years old.

    Those are the years you're in your prime.

386. I am glad that you want to hear a pun about ghosts.

    That's the spirit

387. I'd never let my children watch the orchestra.

   There is too much sax and violins.

388. Did you hear about the human cannonball?

   » It was too bad he got fired.

389. My wife kicked me out because of my terrible Arnold Schwarzenegger impressions.

   But don't worry, I'll be back.

390. Did you hear about the circus that caught on fire?

   » It was in tents.

391. What did the policeman say to the belly button?

   » "You're under a-vest."

392. I used to make clown shoes… which was no small feat.

393. Why don't eggs tell jokes?

    » They'd crack each other up.

394. The one day of the week that eggs are afraid of is Fry-day.

395. Why can't your ear be 12 inches long?

    » Because then it would be a foot.

396. Sleeping comes so naturally to me, I could do it with my eyes closed.

397. What do you call someone with no body and no nose?

    » Nobody knows.

398. Did you hear the rumor about butter?

    Well, I'm not going to spread it.

399. Dad, can you put my shoes on?
    No, I don't think they'll fit me.

400. What did the two pieces of bread say on their wedding day?

    ≫ It was loaf at first sight.

401. Why can't a nose be 12 inches long?

    ≫ Because then it would be a foot.

402. What do you call a gigantic pile of cats?

    ≫ A meow-tain.

403. This graveyard looks overcrowded. People must be dying to get in.

404. **What kind of music do planets like?**

   » Neptunes.

405. **What concert costs just 45 cents?**

   » 50 Cent featuring Nickelback

406. **What lights up a soccer stadium?**

   » A soccer match.

407. **Why did the math book look so sad?**

   » Because it held inside itself so many problems.

408. **I lost an electron.**

   » Are you positive?

409. What do you call cheese that isn't yours?

　》 Nacho cheese.

410. What did the plumber say to the singer?

　》 Nice pipes.

411. What kind of shoes do ninjas wear?

　》 Sneakers

412. This is my step ladder.
I never knew my real ladder.

413. How does a penguin build its house?

　》 Igloos it together.

414. If Apple made a car, would it have Windows?

415. **What did the lead band singer call his twin daughters?**

   » Anna one, Anna two

416. **Why couldn't the toilet paper cross the road?**

   » It got stuck in a crack.

417. **How did Darth Vader know what Luke got him for his birthday?**

   » He felt his presents.

418. **How do fish get high?**

   » Seaweed

419. **Why did the octopus beat the shark in a fight?**

   » Because it was well armed.

420. I asked my trusty reliable dog what three minus three was.

   My dog looked back up at me and said nothing.

421. How much does a hipster weigh?

   » An Instagram.

422. Why did Novak Djokovic pay for his flight to Australia with a Mastercard?

   » Because his Visa didn't work.

423. I used to really hate facial hair… but then it grew on me.

424. How was Rome split in two?

   » With a pair of Ceasars.

425. **Why are plants so thin?**

   » They are light eaters.

426. **I decided to sell my vacuum cleaner because it was just gathering dust.**

427. **What cheese can never be yours?**

   » Nacho cheese.

428. **There's a new type of broom out, it's sweeping the nation.**

429. **I only seem to get sick on weekdays. spoiler I must have a weekend immune system.**

430. **What did mommy spider say to baby spider?**

   » You spend too much time on the web.

431. **What is an arsonist's favorite holiday?**

    » The 4th of July.

432. **The shovel was a groundbreaking invention.**

433. **Did you hear the rumor about butter?**

    Well, I'm not going to spread it!

434. **My wife and I foolishly let astrology get between us. ……. It Taurus apart.**

435. **What do you call someone with no body and no nose?**

    » Nobody knows.

436. **People are usually shocked when they find out… I'm a bad electrician.**

437. I don't trust stairs.
They're always up to something.

438. Why can't you send a duck to space?

    》 Because the bill would be astronomical.

439. What is brown and sticky?

    》 A stick.

440. I once got fired from a juice bottling factory.
Apparently, I couldn't concentrate.

441. You know, people say they pick their nose, but I feel like I was just born with mine.

442. Thinking of having my ashes stored in a glass urn. Remains to be seen.

443. Do you know where you can get chicken broth in bulk?

    » The stock market.

444. I hope to have a great joke about construction,
    but I am still working on it.

445. My cat was just sick on the carpet, I don't think it's feline well.

446. Why were they called the "dark ages"?

    » Because there were a lot of knights.

447. I had a neck brace fitted for me years ago and I've never looked back since.

448. Have you ever heard of a music group called Cellophane?

    » They mostly wrap.

449. My son told me he didn't understand cloning.
I told him, 'That makes two of us.'

450. Pig puns are so boaring.

451. I just saw my wife trip and fall while carrying a laundry basket full of ironed clothes.
I watched it all unfold.

452. Why couldn't the dead car drive into the cluttered garage?

    ⟫ Lack of vroom.

453. I made a playlist for hiking. It has music from Peanuts, the Cranberries, and Eminem. ……….

    I call it my trail mix.

454. **What do you do when balloons fall and are hurt?**

    » You helium.

455. **I am an expert at picking leaves and heating them in water.
It's my special tea.**

456. **My favorite time on the clock is 6:30. Hands down.**

457. **The hat says to the other,
"You stay here, I'll go on a head."**

458. **Why are skeletons, such bad liars?
You can see right through them.**

459. Observer: That's a pretty good ceiling.
Builder: It's not the best, but it's up there.

460. How many tickles does it take to make an octopus laugh?

    ≫ Ten tickles.

461. Why do old plumbers only clean sewer lines during the day?

    ≫ It's because they can't see sh!t at night.

462. What's green and smells like red paint?

    ≫ Green paint.

463. Sore throats are a pain in the neck.

464. When the scientist wanted to clone a deer, he bought a doe it yourself kit.

465. When two vegans get into an argument, is it still called a beef?

466. If I have leftover food at a restaurant and the waiter asks,
'Do you want a box for that?'
I always respond, 'I'm not much of a boxer, but I'll wrestle you for it.'
They never laugh.

467. I will never tell my accountant a joke again.
He just depreciates them.

468. If you wear cowboy clothes, are you ranch dressing?

469. Why did Hitler wear eye glasses?
Because without them he could Nazi.

470. I was addicted to the hokey pokey, but I turned myself around.

471. What do you call a cow with no back legs?

    » An utter drag!

472. I feel sorry for the shopping carts.
They're always getting pushed around.

473. Did you know that if a piano falls on you, your head will B-flat?

474. I was disappointed in the museum.
The display of still-life art was not at all moving.

475. What do you call a cow with no legs?

    ≫ Ground beef

476. On Halloween, October is nearly Octover.

477. The safe was invented by a cop and a robber.
It was quite a combination.

478. The Halloween tale of the haunted refrigerator was chilling.

479. Knock, knock.
Who's there?
Water.
Water who?
Water you asking so many questions for, just open up!

480. Why do crabs never share their lobsters?

    » They are shellfish.

481. What's a vampire's favorite ship?

    » A blood vessel.

482. Do you want to hear a joke about trickle-down economics?
The majority of you won't get it.

483. There's only one thing I can't deal with, and that's a deck of cards glued together.

484. **What do Japanese monsters like to eat?**

   》 Raw-men

485. **"Knock, knock."**
   "Who's there?"
   "Nobel."
   "Nobel who?"
   "Nobel, so I just knocked."

486. **What do you call a happy cowboy?**

   》 A Jolly Rancher.

487. **Son:** Dad, I'm hungry.
   Dad: Hi hungry, I'm Dad.

488. **Why did the Invisible Man decline the job offer?**

   》 He couldn't see himself doing it.

489. What do you call a fancy seafood meal?

   » So-fish-ticated.

490. Why are the boy mushrooms always invited to parties?

   » They're fungis.

491. My son's fourth birthday was today.
   When he came to see me, I didn't recognize him at first.
   I had never seen him be four.

492. Why is organic chemistry the meanest science?
   It's constantly pushing electrons around.

493. "Knock, knock."
   "Who's there?"
   "Ayatollah."
   "Ayatollah who?"
   "Ayatollah you already."

494. **The guy who stole my diary died yesterday.
My thoughts are with his family.**

495. **Why did the banana go to the hospital?**

    » He wasn't peeling well.

496. **I recently went to the "World's Tiniest Wind Turbine" exhibit.
Honestly, not a big fan**

497. **Why do plants hate math?**

    » It gives them square roots

498. **What do you call a cow with legs on only one side?**

    » Lean beef

499. **What do you call a pig that knows karate?**

    » A pork chop.

500. **A friend of mine is known for sweeping girls off their feet.**

   ≫ He's an extremely aggressive janitor.

501. **Where do cinnamon rolls rise?**

   ≫ In the yeast.

502. **Where do you learn to make banana splits?**

   ≫ In sundae school

503. **Why should you always knock before opening the fridge?**

   You never know when a salad will be dressing.

504. **What is a mummy's favorite food?**

   ≫ Wraps

505. **What kind of jokes do you tell during quarantine?**

Inside jokes

506. **What kind of fruit do you bring while sailing?**

Naval oranges

507. **What did the Dalmatian say after lunch?**

» That hit the spot!

508. **How do billboards talk?**

» Sign language

FunLifeNow

Blending
Books, Art, and Fun

Printed in Great Britain
by Amazon